The Worry Box

Suzanne Chiew

Sean Julian

LITTLE TIGER
LONDON

High up on his thinking spot, Murray Bear
looked out across the valley.
"Here you are!" called his sister, Milly.
"It's time for lunch."
"I'm not hungry," Murray sighed.
"You're always hungry!" giggled Milly.
"Come on, or we'll be late meeting
Alfie at the waterfall."

"I don't want to go!" snuffled Murray.
"What if the waterfall's too LOUD?
What if it's so BIG that I get
whooshed away?"

Milly squeezed Murray tight. "Waterfalls *are* big and loud,"
she said. "But they're also beautiful."

"I won't get whisked away?" asked Murray.

"Not with me to hold your paw," said Milly firmly.

Murray thought for a moment then nodded.

"Sharing worries always makes them feel smaller,"
Milly comforted as they headed for home.

When the very last sandwich was eaten, Milly had a secret
to share.

"This is my worry box," she smiled. "When something's
worrying me, I write it down, then I put it inside."

"Does it make your worries disappear?" asked Murray.

"Not quite," said Milly. "But when my worries are in the
box they don't stop me having fun. Let's make one for you."

"Worries won't stop me!" cheered Murray,
popping his worry in the box and
shutting the lid tight.
    "Ready?" Milly asked.
    "Ready!" nodded Murray.

Skipping along the riverbank, the bears
spotted dragonflies dancing above
their heads.

But soon the river raced faster,
and there was a roar of water ahead.

"Nearly there," said Milly.

"Eeek," Murray squeaked
as they rounded the bend.

There, sparkling in the sunlight, was
the rumbling, tumbling waterfall.

"Wow!" gasped Murray, wiping
the spray from his nose.

Just then, there was a shout from
the rocks.

"It's Alfie!" Milly cheered.

Murray took a deep breath.
"Let's go and play," he decided.
"Last one there gets sploshed!"

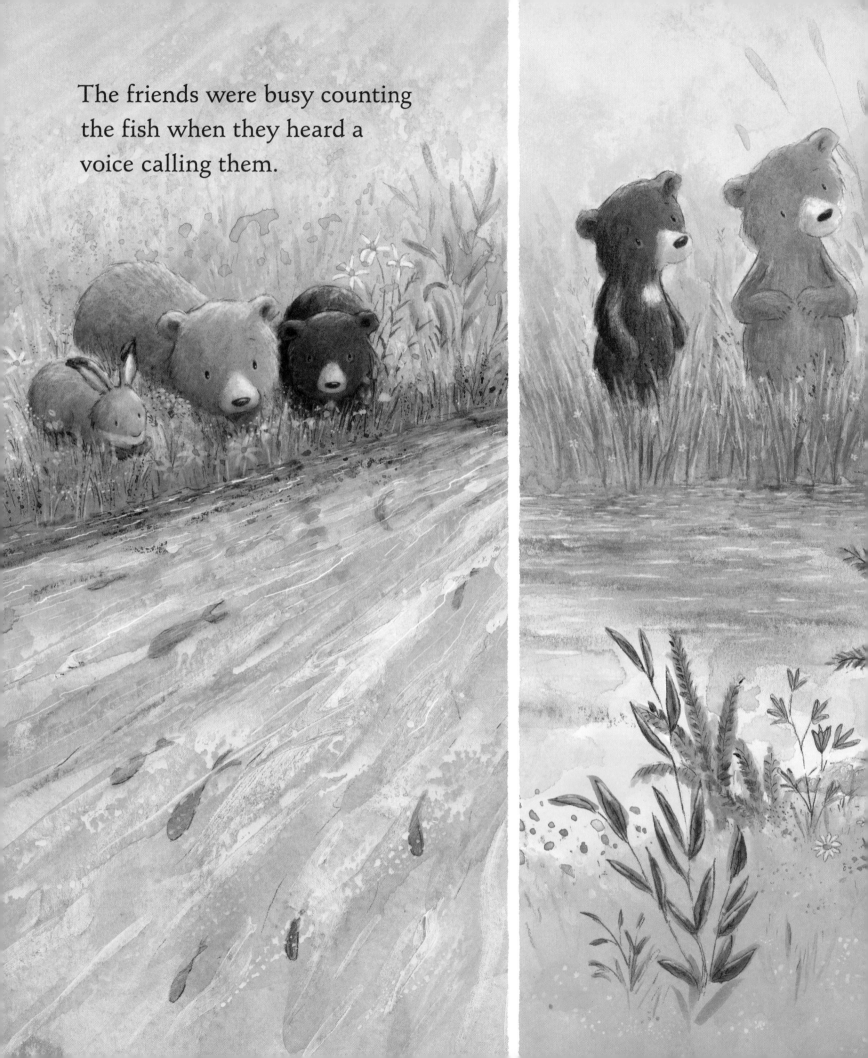

The friends were busy counting
the fish when they heard a
voice calling them.

"Yoo-hoo!" cried a rabbit Murray had never met before.
"It's my cousin, Lara!" beamed Alfie.
Suddenly Murray felt very shy.

Lara scrambled to the top of the rocks.
"I want to go even higher!"
she announced, looking at an oak tree
growing on the bank. "Let's climb
to the top of that!"
The friends raced off.
All except Murray, who
was beginning to worry.

"Oh dear," he sniffed.

Murray wanted to join in but his tummy
felt very tight.

Then he remembered. "My box!" he said.

Quickly he scribbled down his thoughts.

I'm worried that Lara
won't like me.

I'm worried that I'm not
a very good climber.

I'm worried that everyone
will laugh at me.

"Worries won't stop me!" he smiled,
closing the box and trotting
off to the tree.

Up, up, up Murray climbed.
"Come higher!" called Lara. "You can see the sea!"
But Murray had spotted a hole in the trunk.
There, inside, was a nest of fluffy owl chicks!
"Look what I've found, Milly," he whispered.

All afternoon long, the friends played until it was time to go.
"Oh bother," Milly huffed, "I've lost my backpack."

Everyone hunted high and low till they found
the backpack hidden in the reeds.

"Just in time," said Alfie.
"The sun's starting to set."

"Hurry!" Lara squeaked in panic.
"We have to get home!"
　　"Why? What's wrong?" asked Alfie.

Lara's whiskers quivered.

"We won't see where we're going!
 We'll be late for bedtime!
 And . . . and . . . I don't like the dark!"

Murray held Lara's paw. "Sharing worries makes
them feel smaller and less scary," he told her.
"See? I keep mine in a special box."
    He gave her a scrap of paper and a pencil.
"You can put yours in too," Murray smiled.

Lara stayed by Murray's side as they walked through the wood.

"Follow the fireflies," Murray said. "They're like nightlights
to show us the path."

"Eeek!" Lara squeaked as an owl hooted overhead.

"It's OK," whispered Murray. "It's Mr Owl saying 'goodnight'."
Across the treetops the friends heard a hoot in reply.

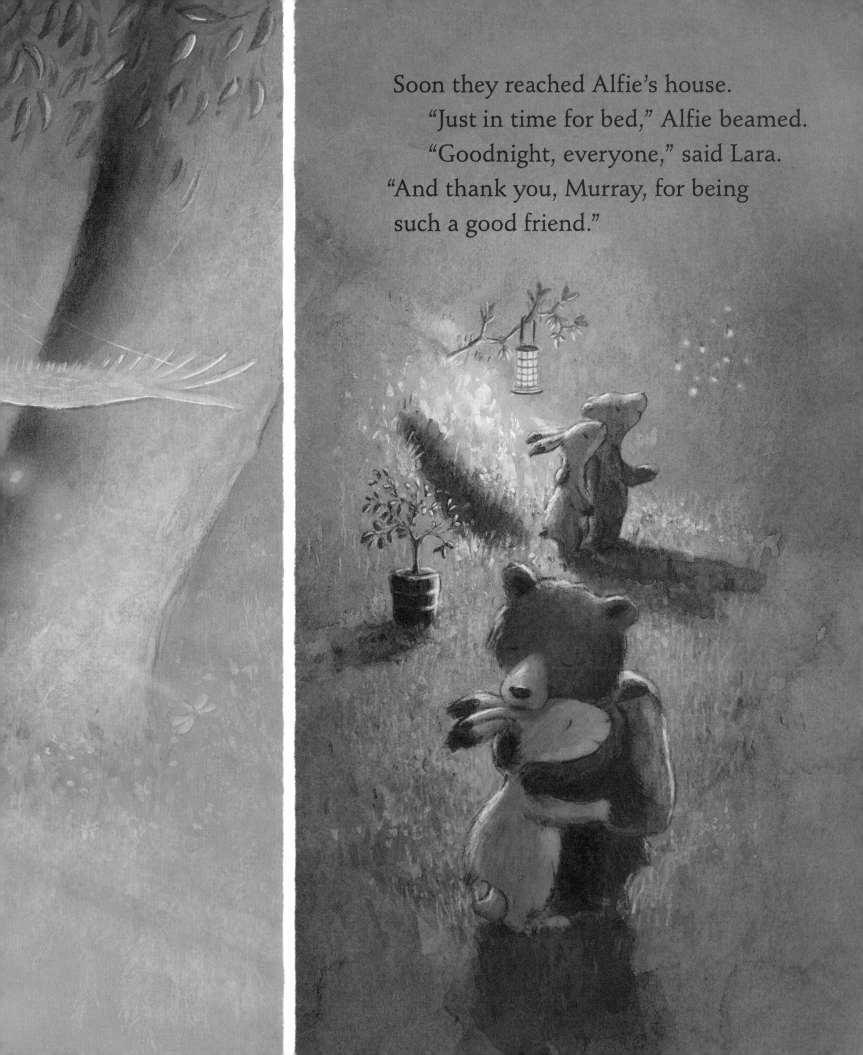

Soon they reached Alfie's house.
    "Just in time for bed," Alfie beamed.
    "Goodnight, everyone," said Lara.
"And thank you, Murray, for being
such a good friend."

High up on his thinking spot, Murray and Milly looked out across the valley.

"Thanks for showing me the waterfall," said Murray.

"It wasn't too big or too loud?" asked Milly.

"It was both!" giggled Murray. "But it was also great FUN! I can't wait until we go again!"